Ho diddle-ho and
A hey diddle-hey,
Weigh the anchor,
We sail today.

Hey diddle-hey,
A ho diddle-ho,
Set the sails...
And off we go!

Ahoy there, first mate Herbie – G.P.J.

Avast ye, young sea dogs Codie and Kyle – G.P.

First published in Great Britain in 2015 by Andersen Press Ltd.,
20 Vauxhall Bridge Road, London SW1V 2SA.

Text copyright © Gareth P. Jones, 2015. Illustration copyright © Garry Parsons, 2015.
The rights of Gareth P. Jones and Garry Parsons to be identified as the author and illustrator
of this work have been asserted by them in accordance with
the Copyright, Designs and Patents Act, 1988.

1 3 5 7 9 10 8 6 4 2
British Library Cataloguing in Publication Data available.
ISBN 978 1 78344 219 5

Colour separated in Switzerland by Photolitho AG, Zürich.
Printed and bound in Malaysia by Tien Wah Press.

Are You The PIRATE CAPTAIN?

GARETH P. JONES   GARRY PARSONS

ANDERSEN PRESS

"This pirate ship be ready," hollered First Mate Hugh. "We've hammered nails, chipped off the snails and even washed the crew."

"We've mopped and swabbed and scrubbed it.
We've cleaned the crow's nest out.
There's one thing though, before we go,
that we can't do without."

"We need a pirate captain to lead us on this trip."

"To make demands, shout out commands, and not take any lip."

Last Sighting of Captain Sid

by First Mate Hugh

"We all recall our last one – that Scurvy Sea Dog Sid.

Never beaten till he got eaten by that giant squid."

The pirates sat there waiting
till First Mate Hugh cried,

"Look!"

"You see that guy
who's rowing by?
His left hand is a hook!"

"Are you the Pirate Captain?
Your hook is quite a sight. Was it a shark
that left its mark in some almighty fight?"

The man said, "I'm no pirate, this here's a pleasure boat."

"And what you took to be a hook is a hanger for my coat."

The next chap had a parrot.
Hugh yelled, "It must be fate!"

"In fact I'll bet
this pirate's pet
will squawk
'Pieces of eight.'"

"Are you the Pirate Captain?"

"Not at all, young fella.
How **absurd!**
It's clear this bird
is part of my **umbrella.**"

Another man came holding
a scroll torn down the fold.

Scurvy Sid's

Gold be in the

"Our missing scrap of treasure map!
It's sure to lead to gold."

"Are you the Pirate Captain -
our map clutched in your fist?"

"This ain't no map,"
replied the chap.
"This here's me
shopping list."

Then in the gloom they spotted
a glistening silver blade,
two gold teeth and underneath
a beard tied in a braid!

"Are you the Pirate Captain?"

"Sadly no, m'hearty.
This pirate gear I'm wearing here
is for a dress-up party."

"But let me help you find one with **courage, brains** and **heart.**"

"You'll need one who will lead your crew and not just look the part."

"Who got this ship all shipshape? Who organised the crew?
Who mopped the sails, removed the snails?"

"Who? I ask you, who?"

The pirates had the answer.
"We know what we must do.
We've all agreed
the one to lead..."

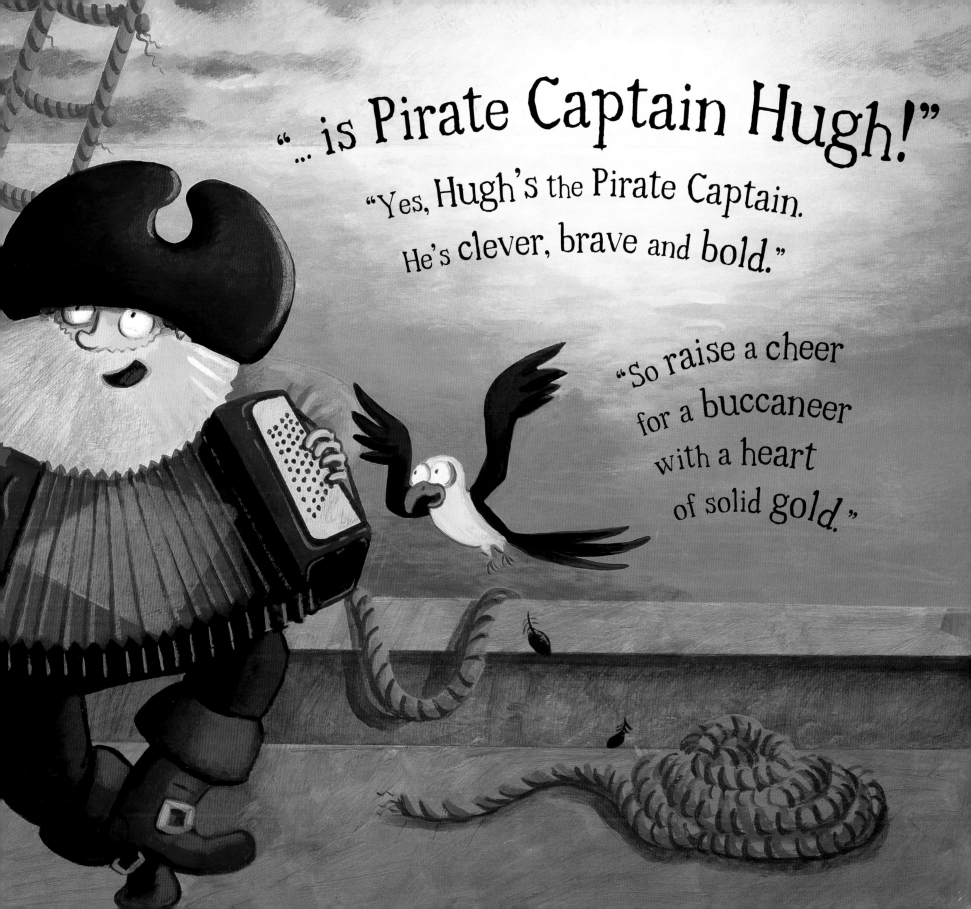